LEGENDS OF SPOOK HOLLOW

MARY L. SHOFKOM

DORRANCE
PUBLISHING CO
EST. 1920
PITTSBURGH, PENNSYLVANIA 15238

Dorrance Publishing Co
585 Alpha Drive
Suite 103
Pittsburgh, PA 15238
Visit our website at *www.dorrancebookstore.com*

ISBN: 979-8-8852-7064-9
eISBN: 979-8-8852-7792-1

LEGENDS OF SPOOK HOLLOW

MARY L. SHOFKOM

In honor of Charlie Snyder, thank you for the inspiration.

A huge thank you to my husband Paul, for supporting me and helping make one of my dreams come true.

Honorable mention to Edward Snyder. Thank you.

Preface

Keep your bravery and your sanity. Spook Hollow is a place to be respected, feared, or maybe just avoided. Curiosity that killed the cat may suggest knowing everything is not essential to sustain a happy, healthy life.

A secret behind every tree, a whisper echoes through the darkness, Fear — a four-letter word to be taken seriously. Spook Hollow is more than just an evil place; it's a presence that exists in the back of one's mind, only to be brought forth by their conscience screaming, "This isn't real." Enjoy these legends and if you begin to doubt their reality, look long and hard into your mirror. Can you see the dark space behind your eyes? Do you know what lurks in those empty places? Be afraid. Spook Hollow exists as surely as your reflection looks back at you.

Introduction

LEGEND - AN INVARIABLE STORY handed down from the past.

Different legends have been passed down from generation to generation. True believers have carried on this tradition to a new era. Spook Hollow's legacy of mystery and death have scared some and intrigued others.

The Legend of Spook Hollow and Beyond

THE LEGEND BEGINS at a very real place in the back hills of Penfield, Pennsylvania. The pureness of the land is original. The mountain terrain is wild and free from human intervention. Trees are intertwined with rock and foliage to create a calm with nature.

Spook Hollow earned its name during a time when Daniel Boone walked a path on this earth. A wooden path leads the way to the mouth of Spook Hollow. The trees seemed to give warning as they grab frantically at your clothes as you enter its threshold. An uneasy feeling washes over anyone who dares to enter. The birds flying above the hollow have no song. They will not penetrate the trees to rest on their branches in this evil place.

A bubbling stream rushes over rock and stone but has no sound. The peculiar stream runs twist and turns, but like magic, the water that touches its right bank runs fresh and sweet while the rushing water that flows to the left bank is of salt water. No fish can survive in the strange waters of Spook Hollow. You can see a strong wind bend each tree to its will. Branches snap back and forth in a violent fit of rage, but you cannot hear their leaves rustle. When the wind is calm and the trees are still, a single fern stands quietly at attention with only one vein protruding the silence. The vein twirls mutely around and around in a hypnotizing dance.

Spook Hollow runs its unexplainable horror through an eight-mile, sharply cut valley. The hollow is protected on both sides by sandstone boulders and rough mountain terrain. The lay of the land leaves an unwelcome sense of danger to any who dare challenge its existence.

Trapper Dan in Spook Hollow

GRANDPA CHARLIE BROUGHT the family to Camp Mountain Run in the early fall of 1890. Gramps ran a Boy Scout camp for the Bucktail Council of Clearfield County. Camp Mountain Run was nestled deep in the mountains of Pennsylvania. The camp was a retreat for Boy Scouts around the United States.

A weary moon descended slowly from the star filled sky. Gramps watched as the sun peeked over the horizon. A smile creased his face with the anticipation of the busy day ahead. It was late afternoon when the Boy Scouts began to arrive at the camp. Cabins were assigned and details given. Each troop ascended to their designated spots. The boys went to unpack and get set for dinner with their troop leader. Tomorrow would be when all the campers would come together.

As night fell, the glow of lanterns reflecting their light through cabin windows gave the camp a homey feel. As the boys nestled into their banks, a hush settled over the camp.

A new day had dawned. The sun shone brightly on the trees of vibrant color. The deep blue sky background gave the hint of a beautiful day ahead. The air was crisp with the scent of fall as the leaves danced around on the ground. Camp Mountain Run would soon be alive with the voices of the scouts as they arose to begin a new adventure.

The smell of bacon frying filtered into the cabins with the anticipation of breakfast. The campers eagerly emerged into the dining hall. Gramps greeted each as they entered, "Good morning." He would repeat several times. The hall was alive with the hum of conversation and laughter; the day had begun.

Many activities had been planned from boating to the archery range, hiking, swimming, and, of course, a survival course. Gramps was in charge of the survival guide. He would begin with the basics of shelter, fire, and then survival foods. Gramps' voice captured his groups attention until he was interrupted by the rumble of a vehicle entering the camp.

The smile on Gramps' face indicated he knew the gentleman approaching him. The two men shook hands as they greeted one another. After a short conversation, Gramps introduced the tall man with red hair as Ranger Jack. The ranger had stopped to ask a favor of Gramps. He was checking the whereabouts of an old trapper that should have walked off the mountain and into town about a month ago. Ranger Jack explained that the man's name was Trapper Dan, and he lived in the mountains all his life. The old trapper had built a log cabin three and a half miles north of the Boy Scout camp. Trapper Dan would travel to town about every three months to replenish his supplies at Morelli's General Store. The ranger figured him to be overdue and in need of essentials. He asked Gramps if he could spare a few men and if Gramps himself would join him in a search up the valley to check on the old trapper.

Grandpa Charlie hesitated only for a moment, remembering the ranger's directions of three and a half miles north of the scout camp. Gramps knew Trapper Dan's cabin would be in Spook Hollow. Caution thrown aside, a group of men were gathered to begin the search for the trapper. All began the search with high hopes and good intentions of finding Trapper Dan hard at work tanning a large supply of hides.

Conversation was light as the group traveled along the wooded path. Laughter echoed between the sandstone throughout the valley drop off. Gramps knew they were about to enter the mouth of Spook Hollow. Ranger Jack was also aware of the stories told about the hollow. Jack wasn't sure if he believed all he was told about this place that some feared.

As the group crossed the threshold of the hollow, the tree branches began to grab at their clothes. The wind softly whispered go back. The temperature seemed to increase by at least 20 degrees. The air was heavy and hard to breathe. The mood of the men had changed from carefree to cautious and guarded. Silence fell over the group of men as they continued closer to Trapper Dan's cabin and deeper into Spook Hollow.

Gramps broke the silence with his booming voice. "Stay alert!" he said. The sudden sound made the men physically jump. "We are getting close," Jack replied. Gramps noticed as the group walked, they were stepping on fallen branches in their path. Their footsteps carried no sound. He could see birds flying high above the treetops, but not down among them. There were no signs of life; not even a bug or a spider could be seen. Soon, they would be upon the cabin but not fast enough. The group of men stopped on the rise looking down on the trapper's cabin. They had arrived.

Trapper Dan's cabin was set on a hillside with large boulders of stone scattered all around. The one room cabin stood surrounded by pine trees and scrub brush. The pine trees dipped their branches low, scraping the side of the cabin. Mud was tightly packed between each cut log. There was a wooden water barrel set on the front corner of the cabin. A small porch was built with an inviting rocking chair perched upon it. There was no sign of life within their sights, no smoke coming from the large stone chimney, and no lights shown through the windows. The group of men quietly circled around the cabin. The solid log front door was closed tightly. Ranger Jack and Gramps stepped up on the porch and knocked on the door, calling out to the trapper, "Dan, it's Jack and Charlie." With no response, the two men opened the door. Cobwebs blocked the doorway and windows. A thick layer of dust covered all of its contents. The stone fireplace had a cast iron pot hanging over a deep layer of spent coals. In the pot appeared to be what they thought was dried up stew. On the table was a place setting for one, a cup, one plate, and one fork. A rock-hard molded loaf of bread remained on the plate in the center of the table. Gramps and the ranger exchanged a concerned look. Both men decided to exit the cabin and search for some clues that could lead them to the whereabouts of the old trapper or an explanation of what took place there.

The volunteers spread out, looking for signs of an explanation. Gramps noticed there were no traps or skins anywhere. A strange, eerie feeling pulled at Gramp's senses. The hair on the back of his neck stood; a chill ran through his body causing him to shiver. Something strange had happened here. After completing their search, the men gathered at the front of the cabin. Murmurs of concern filled the air. The somberness of the group was evident. They all agreed something was amiss with their surroundings.

Now anxious to leave there, the group looked to Gramps for direction. Gramps suggested a different path towards home might give them clues to trap or Dan's whereabouts. Ranger Jack agreed. Hopefully they would find some answers.

Gramps led the way; the new trail was of rougher terrain with limited sight distance. Loose gravel made their footing unsure. The group of men eagerly began their descent down the mountainside. Carefully, the group climbed over sandstone rock and slipped on gravel. Gramps again noticed stones and gravel tumbling downward had no sound. Unsure if any other had noticed this unnatural event, he viewed each face of the volunteers. Their eyes were wide with questioning uncertainty. Without saying a word, the band of men continued their search towards home.

The silence was broken like shattering glass. "Over here," one of the volunteers yelled. He pointed towards an object half buried in the trail. The group formed a circle around the area. Gramps knelt and carefully began unearthing the object by brushing the dirt and gravel from it.

Ranger Jack now knelt beside Gramps. A single worn tan buckskin moccasin lay between them. The weathered moccasin had been torn with several slashes down the one side. Ranger Jack identified it as belonging to trapper Dan. He remembered a sunny day when trapper boasted about the new moccasins, he had made for himself, showing them off to the folks at Morelli's store. Jack pulled up the moccasin and placed it in his backpack. Only moments had passed when another shout of discovery gathered their attention. Again, the group assembled towards the point of interest. A rusty, twisted piece of steel partly embedded in the stump of a tree had the attention of all. Gramps and Jack together worked to free the object from its prison. Upon examination, Gramps declared it to be an animal trap. Ranger Jack spoke as he packed the steel trap in his backpack, "Let's spread out." The group of men dispersed in all directions. The search continued, but almost immediately, one in the group announced his find; two more would claim a find in their direction. All the same discoveries were of steel traps, some twisted, some bent, but all destroyed. With everything gathered and put in the backpack the band of volunteers moved on. Gramps came upon a trapper's basket; it had been crushed flat and its contents scattered about and destroyed. A feeling of dread weighed heavily on Gramps. "Quickly gather everything," Grandpa told the group. The group of men, now on edge, collected all that was found. Once again, they began their way home, the threat of darkness upon them only heightening their fears. The group maneuvered the rough terrain over boulders and shrubs at increased speed. No one wanted to be out there after nightfall. The hollow was more alive with movement all racing the sun. A man out in front of the group came to a sudden stop. He had said not a word but stared at the ground in front of his feet, his face drained of color, eyes wide with fright; he only pointed a finger, drawing attention to what he had found. Everyone gathered near the man, all eyes following him. Ranger Jack slowly approached with caution. He knelt on one knee with apprehension as he lifted a worn, tan buckskin moccasin. A perfect match to the one found earlier; however, this moccasin contained a leg bone. The leg bone appeared to be severed at the knee. The upper bone bleached white from the sun. In silence, the remains were placed in the backpack. Jack stood with a sigh, looked at Gramps, and motioned for the search party to move on.

Nothing more was ever found of Trapper Dan; his fate continues to be a mystery unsolved. One can only speculate Trapper Dan's existence was wiped out by something unnatural only in Spook Hollow. Forces of evil cannot be explained. Truth or imagination? Truth is of great value; imagination is a gift...or is it?

The Tin Can

EARLY IN THE SPRING of 1891, snow slowly melted from the kiss of a warming sun. The streams ran swift and full over silt and stone. Trees burst with the promise of new life. Magic filled the air with songs of the blue jay and sparrow. A renewed spirit danced on a soft breeze. Springtime in the mountains was a breathtaking experience.

Gramps and his son, Pete, were planning a day of fishing. The next day would be the beginning of a successful trout season and Gramps and Pete would be ready. They stared at a detailed map of Clearfield County. The map, complete with mountain terrain rivers and streams, lay flat on the wooden table. They chose a promising stream running through a winding valley. To get to the spot of good fishing, a trail would lead them through a place called Spook Hollow. Gramps expressed his concern, just short of fright, not wanting to enter the wicked place. Several alternate routes were tracked on the map to go around the hollow that would take a day or more of travel on foot. Reluctantly, Gramps agreed to pass through the hollow, only as quickly as possible.

Gramps again studied the map closely. He charted the most direct route to the stream; they would leave before the sun made its appearance.

Gramps, having a rough night's sleep, was up early to cook breakfast. Pete awoke to the smell of bacon, eggs, and hot coffee. Eager to be on their way, they enjoyed their food quickly and gathered their supplies.

Pete was a strong man, rugged and athletically built. He, being the most capable of physical strength, chose to carry the trapper's basket full of supplies.

The fishermen traveled about three and a half miles before entering the northern section of the strange valley. The sleepy sun approached the horizon to form a milky gray hue. This time of day made everything appear simple as if black and white. The forest awoke in slow motion. Quiet, with only their boots marking the muddy path could be heard.

Talk was light and consisted of stories of days past. A big buck that outsmarted all, the turkey with the impressive beard, or the fish that got away.

Pete and Gramps were eager to begin the day's catch. Neither one noticed a strange silence as their muddy boots no longer carried a sound. They traveled uphill around brush and rock. The climb became rough, unaware of nature's caution. The brush tangled in their feet as if trying to stop them. Tree branches bent down in their faces to wave warning.

Pete was the first one going up the rugged trail. Gramps was about ten paces behind; without warning, Pete suddenly stopped and turned to Gramps. Pete's face now of ash color, eyes wide with fright, a fear so strong Gramps himself felt its presence. Pete could neither speak nor run. By driving force, he was pushed down to one knee. He was being shoved to the ground, but by what? Gramps ran to Pete. He pulled frantically on his arm all the while yelling for Pete to fight. "Pete, get up!" Gramps yelled. Pete looked helplessly at Gramps, as if to say, "Help me!" Gramps was powerless against the unseen force. He could do nothing to help his son. The evil energy seemed to feed on the terror it instilled. Gramps looked around for help, something, anything. Then like a flood, recognition of an earlier time at about the same place memories came rushing back. Gramps turned to Pete. "Get out of the pack! Get out of the pack now, get it off! Hurry Pete!" Gramps yelled. With the last of his strength, Pete worked his arm around until he freed himself from the pack. Pete was up, running into Gramps' arms. They watched in awe as the trapper's basket was crushed before their eyes. Its contents, air-bound and thrown everywhere by an unseen force. Pete had seen enough. He urged Gramps to run. Down the mountainside they ran, feet taking flight towards safety, not stopping until they felt the warmth of the sun upon their face. Gramps had to stop, his lungs on fire and straining for a breath. Pete was on guard, eyes constantly moving and looking behind them but not wanting to see what it was. Pete spoke first. "What was that?" Gramps, now looking over Pete's appearance asked, "Are you alright?"

Pete just nodded and stared at Gramps with unanswered questions. "We'll talk later, let's keep moving," Gramps replied.

Once in the safety of their own home, they sat at the kitchen table. Gramps explained what he remembered about Trapper Dan and his trapper basket that was destroyed. What was out there had a pure hatred for those baskets. There was no explanation for Trapper Dan's disappearance or for what horror that just took place that day.

Pete, unsatisfied with no explanation, let the happenings of that day fester. He paced back and forth, unable to settle his churning emotions. He needed answers. Pete had an idea. He rummaged through an old box, pulling out a large tin can. He wrote the date and his name on the inside of the can. Pete wrote $25 on the bottom of the can. He took the can upstairs to show Gramps. Gramps was perched on his favorite stool on the front porch. Pete explained he couldn't shake what had taken place earlier that morning. "Some things are better off not knowing," Gramps replied. Still, Pete would tell of his idea. He wanted to hang the tin can from a tree trunk at the place where the occurrence happened. The point of the can was to see if another person could go there or if the horrifying experience was Pete's alone. Any person presenting the can back to Pete would be paid the $25.

After much discussion, Gramps knew Pete would not rest until an attempt for answers was made. It was agreed upon. The two again entered the valley on the same repeated trail, this time without a trapper's basket. Pete was nervous, his brow wet with sweat. Both men alert to their surroundings, they reached the area without incident. Quickly, the tin can was wired to a tree. Pete saw the destroyed trapper basket he had worn over his shoulder earlier that morning. A chill ripped through his body. With their feat accomplished, the retreat home was quick moving.

Pete and Gramps would repeat their story at Mereili's General Store. They knew the challenge would be accepted eagerly.

From time to time, stories of another attempt would be heard from another victim. No one has ever been able to claim the prize money to prove the truth of the legend. You could attempt to retrieve the tin can; just remember, if you dare go, don't bring a trapper's basket. It remains unclaimed, although there are signs of others who have tried...and failed.

Ghost of the White Dog

IT WAS A VERY COLD NIGHT. The moon was round, full, and bright, with the clearness you could see a distance. The house was warmed by the glow of the crackling fire. The family was all tucked in their beds; sleep had come early after a hard day. Gramps remained seated in the chair before the fire. He would sleep there tonight, feeding the fire to keep his family warm.

Gramps' eyes were heavy, he could hear the wind whistle through the trees. The warmth of their home made Gramps struggle to remain awake. He would close his eyes only for a moment. Gramps was startled awake, a chilling howl cut through the tranquility of slumber. Gramps jolted to his feet. Again, a painful howl echoed through the moon lit night. The house became alive with commotion. Gramps looked from window to window in hopes of getting a glimpse at whatever created such a noise. Everyone gathered in the kitchen, Gramps turned to see all eyes on him. All talked at once; questions flew from person to person. Gramps raised a hand to quiet the room. Although he had seen nothing, Gramps made reference to a mountain lion in the area. All were satisfied with the explanation. Yawning and eyes burning, they returned to their beds. everyone except Pete. He was old enough to know the sound was not that of a mountain lion.

Pete looked to Gramps with a questioning expression. Gramps had no answers. He had never heard the queer sound before. Throughout the night, they took turns going from window to window,

waiting and watching for the cause. The windows were frosted in each corner; ice crystals formed like glitter on the snow. The remainder of the night was a silent vigil.

In the early morning, all conversation evolved around their rude awakening; Grandma gave the warning talk of safety and mountain lions. Gramps and Pete remained silent until they understood what they were dealing with.

Gramps had given Pete permission to stay home from school. He wanted Pete's help looking for the tracks and maybe a hunt. The others left for school and Grandma busied herself in the kitchen. Gramps and Pete ventured outside in search of an answer to their late-night visitor; they circled the yard around the house, making the circle larger with each pass. Neither could find any tracks in the snow. Puzzled, Gramps told Pete they were heading for town. Merelli's General Store was the main gossip hall of Pennfield. All who had news, or others looking for news, gathered there each day to pass the time. Gramps knew if anyone had heard or seen something amiss, the story would find its way to that spot.

Gramps and Pete listened to all the stories the other men were telling. Their tales were told with conviction. After an hour or so, Gramps cleared his throat to draw the attention towards himself. The group of men looked his way and waited. Gramps wasn't one who talked at these gatherings. He was mostly a listener. Now that he had all eyes on him, he nonchalantly lit his pipe and said, "Did anyone see or hear anything strange last night?" The group of men were quiet on the edge of their seats and waiting for an explanation. One by one, they shook their heads no. They looked at each other, confirming they all agreed. Gramps continued on with a story about his night. He described the eerie howl, and he talked about looking for tracks and finding the snow undisturbed. Suggestions made by the group varied from maybe a screech owl to maybe a bobcat, yet no one could offer an explanation as to why there were no tracks in the snow. After much conversation and little explanation, an agreement was reached to scout around the mountain, ask questions, and meet again later in the week.

Gramps and Pete drove home as they discussed all the events that had taken place. They decided to keep all concerns to themselves. Gramps didn't want to worry Grandma or the other kids.

A plan was made to outsmart their visitor. That night, the two set up looking out the windows waiting to hear that sound. The sound that left so many questions. There were no strange sounds, no sightings of...of...of whatever they were waiting for. As the night stillness took over, Pete fell asleep at the kitchen table. His head was tilted to one side, and a soft, steady breathing sound escaped from his lips. Gramps drank coffee and listened to Pete's peaceful slumber. Gramps would keep watch tonight, alone.

With the sun, came the start of a new day. Pete was angry at himself for falling asleep. Gramps looked very tired. He would take a nap this afternoon. Pete went on to school. When he came home from a long day of book learning, he hurried to talk to Gramps about their next move. The two decide to sit up again and wait. Pete was determined to remain awake this time.

The lights turned low and their voices at a whisper, Gramps and Pete patiently waited. It was 1:00 a.m. Pete announced that he was going to give up and go to bed. He laid in his bed frustrated and tired, but he couldn't sleep. He tossed and turned in his bed. Gramps paced a worn spot on the old wooden floor. The wall clock kept time with a steady tick tock. Pete began to doze off. Gramps became tired with his pacing; his legs and feet were heavy.

It was about 2:30 in the morning when, without warning, the long-awaited howl ripped through the silence of the night. Pete jumped to his feet and ran to his bedroom window. Gramps pushed the kitchen curtains aside, trying to see what was responsible for the sound. The night was clear and cold. The moon shining bright gave the snow a luster of dancing diamonds. There in the backyard stood what appeared to be a large white wolf. The majestic creature moved across the ground with such grace that they couldn't tell if it walked or floated. As the men watched the animal disappear into the border of the pine trees, Pete ran for the door, pulling on his boots with one hand and grabbing his gun with the other. Gramps met Pete at the door. "I think we should wait until morning to hunt this one. We will wait until daylight. We don't know anything about that animal, there are too many questions," Gramps said.

At first light, the two hunters headed for the backyard. To their amazement, not a hint of the visitor could be found. Again, there were no tracks, markings, or impressions disturbing the fluffy white ground cover. Disappointed, they returned to the house.

That afternoon, Gramps returned to MereIli's store. A game of checkers had the attention of the crowd on the enclosed front porch. After casual hellos, Gramps stood, leaning against a log post. Two men argued about the rules of the game. Gramps calmly announced that he heard the howl again. This time, he had seen what made the sound. Gramps had their undivided attention; all eyes were on him. "Well?" a man's voice boomed out. "It was a white wolf, a big one, but when Pete and I went to track him, the animal left no tracks, no marks, no disturbances in the snow," said Gramps. The men began to all talk at once. The ruckus continued for a short time. Mr. Smith stepped out of the store onto the porch. He told Gramps that he could help him to understand what he had seen and heard. Everyone stopped talking and stared at the two men.

Mr, Smith wasn't much of a talker. On days when he would come to the store, he would buy his necessities and quickly leave, but today he was the center of attention. Mr. Smith drew in a deep breath. He looked down at the boards on the porch. "I can tell you the story of the White Dog." he said.

The Legend of White Dog

THE YEAR WAS SAID TO BE around 1870. Lance sat at his camp-fire heating a pot of strong coffee. Lance's only companion was a large, pure white canine. His name was simply, "Dog." Dog laid quietly at Lance's side. He appeared to be asleep, but his senses were keenly aware that they were about to have visitors. Dog sprang to his feet with a low warning growl that cut through the dark silence. Lance, knowing his comrade well, reached slowly for his gun. Lance began to hear the steady drumming of horse hooves beating a path toward his camp when the horses came to a stop, they were close. Lance could see two men on horseback on the outskirts of the camp's fire light. The two men slowly began to climb down off their saddles. An unmistakable sound of the hammer of a gun being pulled back stopped them in mid-air. Lance spoke to them in a low, even tone. "Can I help you gents?" After some tense conversation, Lance decided that the two men were harmless, just cattle drivers on the way home after a long drive.

The three men circled around the campfire for warmth. Coffee and beef jerky were shared all around. Now the company was a real treat for Lance. This had been a long trip. During the last two weeks, Lance's only conversation was one-sided with his white dog.

After the men had warmed themselves and filled their stomachs, they unrolled their beds and turned in for the night.

Morning was close even though darkness still filled the sky. The white dog again sounded a warning of approaching horses. Dust flew as eight men rode into camp with their guns drawn. Lance and his new companions jumped to their feet, reaching for their own guns. It was too late; the posse had surprised the sleeping men. Lance discovered all too late that his late-night companions were in fact wanted horse thieves.

Lance tried to explain the chain of events, leading up to his acquaintance of the other two. He didn't know these outlaws and he was no horse thief. The posse saw Lance's explanation as an attempt to clear himself. They figured he would lie to prove his innocence. No man wanted to hang. The posse were roughneck, loudmouth, townsmen, fueled on by cheap whiskey and the repugnant smell of blood. Their tempers were egged on by an overweight cow hand whose reputation was not far from the two men who stood accused beside Lance. "Let's hang 'em now," the man roared. A cheer echoed throughout the posse. Lance was violently shoved to the ground. White Dog leaped and stood in front of Lance. White Dog's legs were positioned and his back crouched, ready to spring into action to defend his friend and master. Lance yelled for White Dog to run. He knew the posse was eager for blood. Dog ran hard, leaping over rock and sage brush. Some of the men in the posse aimed and fired at the white dog, but no bullets found their target.

Dog ran to the mountaintop and watched as a group of men circled around his master. Dog obeyed Lance always and this time would be no different.

The posse on edge, caught up in the feel of authoritative power made them in no mood to wait on a judge and jury. The thrill of the hunt and rush of adrenaline gave death an exciting ending to a long chase. A rope was thrown over an apple tree branch. A yell of excitement erupted from the group of men. "Hang the horse thieves," was chanted in the wind. White Dog watched from the mountaintop, unable to help his friend and master.

Lance repeated his plea of not guilty. "You can't hang an innocent man," Lance yelled out. The posse hung the first horse thief. The rope jerked and the dead man swung from side to side. The second horse thief begged and pleaded with the posse, but his pleas fell on deaf ears. The rope jerked again, and a second man gasped for breath, his legs jerked and spasmed, his face turned red and then purple, then no more struggle. His limp body swung, unchallenged. his corpse was dropped to the ground in one swift motion. The group of men cheered and shouted for one more outlaw to swing.

Lance was roughly grabbed and thrown high up on a horse's back. His hands were tied behind his back and a rope put around his neck. He glared at the posse with fire in his eyes. "I'm not a horse thief," he said calmly. "If you hang me, an innocent man, and put my body in the back of that wagon, to prove my innocence to you, your horses will not be unable to pull my corpse across that trout stream." A hush fell over the posse as they contemplated what Lance had said. A thunderous laugh erupted from the makeshift lawman. Lance could feel White Dog's eyes on him. He knew his friend watched helplessly. Lance looked to the mountain top to see his friend. A slap and the horse that Lance was sitting on ran from its abuser. The second Lance died, White Dog lifted his snout and howled loud and long. Another howl rang out, then silence.

Lance's limp body was laid beside the two horse thieves in the back of the wooden wagon. The posse now quiet that the fun was over. They were in a hurry to get to the saloon. The wagon rumbled through a clearing; the bridge was in sight. The law man joked about the last words Lance had said, but when the horses approached the stream, they became restless and hard to control. The driver slapped the reins and urged the horse on, but they could not, or would not move forward. The driver took out his whip and mercilessly beat the animals. The horse reared and whinnied, but still could not cross the bridge. Another man tried leading the horses across but could not get them to move. After 15 minutes, the horses stood, sweaty and confused. The posse became nervous; they quietly talked between themselves, remembering what Lance had told them.

Two men took Lance's body out of the wagon. The driver yelled a go-ahead to the horses. They moved with ease across the bridge. Lance's body had to be carried across. In the distance, they heard the reminding howl of White Dog. Stone-faced, the men realized they had hung an innocent man.

Still, today, if you listen really close, you can hear the howl of an injustice that was done.

"So, you see," Mr. Smith said in a whisper, "White Dog roams the night looking for his master and friend. You won't find any tracks because there aren't any. The animal is the spirit of injustice."

Sighting of White Dog's Ghost

THE MORNING HOUR had come. A rooster announced the arrival of the sun. The air was cool, a thick, white mist clung at the ground. Dawn of the day was calming, a not dark but not light sky.

Grandma was up early. She would travel to Merrelli's General Store for supplies. she finished her early morning self-routine. The stairs creaked as she descended into the kitchen. Quietly, she put on her boots and coat. She pulled the door closed with a soft click; it latched, ensuring the safety of its occupants inside.

It was a cold morning. With each step, the crusting snow sounded its surrender under Grandma's weight. A whisper could be seen as the words froze, exiting your mouth. The whisper, warm and damp, traveled a short distance until like magic, it disappeared. Grandma always would sing to herself.

Snow lined the roadside, creating a guiding wall to show the way. Grandma traveled at a slow pace, feeling the slip of each tire. Both hands gripped tightly on the steering wheel.

Up ahead, a movement caught her eye. Grandma squinted, slowing the car to almost a stop. There was an abundance of deer searching for food this time of year. Grandma didn't want to hurt one. The headlights of the car pierced through the mist ahead. There stood a large, pure white canine. Its coat was thick and full, almost aglow against the headlights of the car. Grandma stomped on the brakes. The car slid sideways against a bank of snow. Grandma looked out the window. The white dog stood on the opposite side of the road. He posed himself so as to make eye contact. Grandma stared at the sight before her. His front paws were positioned high on the snowbank. A magnificent creature, beautiful but dangerous. The eyes glowed red as the light reflected in them. Grandma couldn't move. She sat in a trance as the proud animal lifted his muzzle to the rising day. Its howling echoed through the valley. Grandma shivered as a chill crept through her. One last glance toward Grandma, an acknowledgment of sorts was understood between eye contact. White Dog's painful howl sounded once more, then he glided across the snowy mist and disappeared from sight. Grandma sat for a few calming minutes with a smile upon her face. She felt privileged to have had the opportunity to witness the legend. She never again was to see White Dog.

Another Sighting of White Dog's Ghost

LES TURNER STAYED IN A CABIN named Glen-a-Vu at Camp Mountain Run. He was in charge of the Boy Scouts camp's swimming pool. He worked there for eight summers. Early, every morning, Turner would leave his cabin and walk across the camp to check the pH levels of the pool. On this particular morning as Turner walked towards the pool, he decided to take a shortcut through the picnic area. The morning dew glistened upon the grass. The sun streaked through the tops of the pine trees, trying to erase the dampness. Turner whistled his favorite tune; you could hear it echo throughout the stillness of the camp.

The camp was quiet early in the morning. Turner was usually the only distraction that penetrated the serene peace. As he turned towards the wooded area heading in the direction of the pool, he saw White Dog statue standing still. White Dog possessed a proudness; he was magnificent. His white coat shone bright with the sun illuminating his presence. Turner froze; he stood watching the animal. White Dog lifted his muzzle high, howling a low, sad sound. It shook Turner's very soul. White Dog looked again at Turner, then repeated the mournful howl. Turner stood almost entranced as the white dog slowly faded from sight. Turner realized he had been holding his breath. He took in a large gasp of air, shook his head, and headed for the mess hall. Turner found Gramps sitting, drinking his coffee. He told Gramps about the white dog, how its sound was sad as if grieving;

he could feel the pain the sound instilled. How could such an exqui-site creature be so mournful? Turner wanted to track him, but Gramps smiled and said, "Les, you can't track a ghost." Les Turner never did see White Dog again.

A New Believer

HAL WAS AN EXECUTIVE for the Bucktail Council. He was a business-type man. He didn't believe in the supernatural or legends. He was a book-smart, pencil pusher from the city, always dressed in a three-piece suit. Sometimes, Hal would be at the camp on business matters, and he would hear legends about Spook Hollow, Trapper Dan, and White Dog. He would laugh them off as kid stories just for entertainment.

One night, around 9:00 p.m., Hal was headed to the camp. He had a meeting with Gramps about expanding Camp Mountain Run. The night had a silver glow from the mixture of clouds and the moon. As Hal traveled closer to his destination, the dirt road became twisted and narrow. Trees lined the roadside and gave a tunneling effect. Hal drove slowly, because he was used to paved, lined roads. Ahead was a sharp turn to the left. As the headlights skimmed the road's edge, they gave a spotlight effect on the dense trees. Once the car made the curve, the headlights stopped. There, standing in the center of the road, was a large, white animal. Hal slammed on his brakes, and the rear of the car fish-tailed back and forth. The car came to a sudden, body throwing, stop. He adjusted his glasses and checked his hands for signs of blood. After being satisfied that there was none, he looked up at the road. White Dog stood tall and never flinched at the oncoming vehicle. Hal locked his doors. He nervously fidgeted with his seatbelt and ran his fingers through his hair, but never took his eyes off the animal. White Dog looked to the stars and gave a low howl, then another. Hal could have wet his pants. His whole body was shaking uncontrollably. He just sat there, staring with both hands on the steering wheel.

After what seemed like an eternity, White Dog penetrated the thick forest with a graceful glide. During the next few minutes, Hal sat there thinking he had imagined the whole thing. The trees and moon light must be playing a trick on him. He smiled to himself and then began to laugh out loud. Hal rolled his window down halfway and yelled, "Ha, ha, you're not out there, it's just the moonlight." As if to answer, a loud, long howl echoed in the distance. Hal rolled his window up as quickly as he could. He put his car in drive and headed as fast as he could go towards camp.

Gramps heard a car coming rapidly up the dirt road. He could hear dirt and rock being thrown by the fast-approaching vehicle. The car came to an abrupt stop. Gramps could see a man jump out, and in a full run, head towards his cabin. Gramps saw that it was Hal; he quickly opened the door, but Hal pushed his way in—still at a run. Hal had a look of bewilderment upon his face. His eyes became huge as he told Gramps of his story. Gramps smiled and patted Hal on the back. He offered him some coffee to help calm him down. White Dog, now, had a new believer.

Hatchet Hands

HIGH ON A MOUNTAIN RIDGE, the Hutchins' pig farm lay nestled among the pine trees. Mr. Hutchins had built their home a mile south of the hollow. The couple had built a successful living. Time took its toll; Mr. Hutchins had become sick. He had lost the battle and left Mrs. Hutchins to herself.

Running a farm alone was exhausting and overwhelming. Time began to take wear; the backside of the large barn was decaying and falling down. The pigpen was in need of repair. Mrs. Hutchins cared for the livestock as best as she could.

One evening, an intense thunderstorm shook the mountain tops. Lightning flashed with a blinding magnitude; winds had picked up force. Rain, light at first, turned torrent. The downpour thundered against the tin rooftops. Mrs. Hutchins climbed out of her comfortable chair; she crossed the room to close the bedroom window. As she reached for the old window crank, a blinding glow of lightning flew across the sky, scattering in several directions creating cracks through the darkness. Again, night became day as lightning illuminated the night's surroundings. Mrs. Hutchins saw what she thought to be a silhouette of a man standing by her pigpen. The flash of light was quick, lasting only a moment. She waited for the next. Again, the darkness was interrupted by light. Mrs. Hutchins' eyes had seen true. The figure stood by the pigpen. She ran for the protection of her shotgun. Checking the chamber, ready to defend, she walked out of her

screen door to the porch. The wind whipped her hair around her face. Her clothing clung tightly to her body, forced there by the anger of the storm.

The rain, now a soft drizzle, but lightning still brightened the night. Mrs. Hutchins could see the figure standing tall. The intruder was wearing a long, grayish-colored cloth tied by a rope at the mid-section. Long, matted hair flew wildly in the wind. The being stood on top of a wash tub turned upside down. He moved his arms above his head one at a time, striking the tin roof of the pigpen as he brought his hands down.

"Get away from my pigs!" Mrs. Hutchins yelled. No answer came, the intruder showed no signs of stopping. She decided to fire off a round to scare him away. The shot rang out loud, echoing through all the night. Startled, the stranger dropped to the ground.

The storm continued; flashes of lightning provided visual confirmation. The intruder was running for protection, disappearing within the trees.

Mrs. Hutchins didn't sleep very well that night. She paced from window to window, watching over her pigs. The storm had passed; the promise of a new day was peeking over the horizon. The widow dressed to prepare herself for a day of hard work. This morning, she would carry her shotgun at her side. Her boots made the familiar mucking sound that gave the pigs a welcoming sign their breakfast was about to be served. The barn became alive with squeals of anticipation. Mrs. Hutchins visually skimmed the area before she propped the shotgun against an empty stall. The feeding complete, she decided to explore the area. Footprints in the mud showed proof of the intruder; oddly, the human-shaped prints were oversized with six toes. Ladder in hand, she approached the pigpen. With a bang, the ladder rested against the structure. Its tin covering, rust in color, had been pounded through. The torn edges were jagged and sharp. Blood had pooled in the caverns of the dented tin. The damage inspected; Mrs. Hutchins worked the morning hours quickly. An

uneasy concern remained; she thought to report the happenings but decided against it. Townspeople might think she was crazy.

Later that afternoon, Mrs. Hutchins heard the familiar rumble of a truck. She pulled the blue, flowered curtains back. It was Grandpa Charlie from the scout camp. Charlie often brought a load of scraps after a weekend jamboree. The feed helped with the care of the pigs, also to protect the camp from hungry bears.

A welcoming grin lit up Mrs. Hutchins face. A smile and wave responded. The scraps unloaded; Gramps climbed the porch steps. Mrs. Hutchins met him there, cup of coffee in hand. She motioned towards a chair for Gramps to rest. After the pleasantries and thank you. Mrs. Hutchins told of the evening before. Grandpa Charlie listened with concern; he, himself, had sightings in the past.

Gramps believed that Hatchet Hands was forced out of his natural home by progress. Route 80 was being built through uninhabited ground; a mountainous area untouched by civilization. The closer the construction equipment pushed, the more frightened Hatchet Hands became. Putting her somewhat at ease, Gramps finished his coffee and continued his way.

Summer was passing in an instant. The days were long and hot. Hundreds of faces passed through Camp Mountain Run. Gramps continued to feed Mrs. Hutchins pigs. Mrs. Hutchins days had been full of hard work; her nights remained quiet and lonely. She hadn't seen Hatchet Hands again. Summer passed without more events.

Autumn was closing in, a beautiful time in the mountains. An array of bright colors intertwined in an autumn collage. The breeze was brisk, carrying a promise of cold weather to come. Geese flew in uniform across the sky, announcing their departure throughout the valley. Gramps welcomed a new wave of Boy Scouts that had just arrived. Voices chatted and scouts explored the grounds, while Gramps spoke to each cabin counselor. The day flew quickly by as the campers unpacked and became acquainted with each other. That night at the mess hall, Gramps stood to greet all. He detailed all the fun they were

to have and outlined the rules. No food left out was stressed; bears would smell it and enter their cabins to claim it.

The camping adventure had gone well. A great time was had, with memories made and new friendships formed. It was time to pack up and head home. Camp cleanup had begun. A particular cabin site in the back of the grounds had left a lot of food waste: bags of chips, cookies, and fruit. Angry at this waste, Gramp threw everything in garbage cans. He knew he would need to make a trip to the pig farm tonight. Gramps cleaned all afternoon. By early evening, he began to load the scrapes in the bed of his truck. Gramps looked around the corner towards the last cabin. Garbage cans lay turned on their sides, and food scraps littered the ground. A glimpse of sudden movement drew Gramps' attention. Running upright was a figure covered in gray, running for protection of the trees. Gramps called after the being, but it did not stop. The grounds were cleaned quickly. Gramps worried about the smell of food inviting bears into the camp. The truck now loaded; Gramps drove toward the Hutchins' pig farm.

Mrs. Hutchins perched on her porch, peeling potatoes. She smiled seeing Gramps jump out of his truck. He climbed the steps and settled on the porch swing. Mrs. Hutchins poured them both a cold glass of iced tea. Gramps told her his sighting of Hatchet Hands. Conversation continued, trying to find an explanation to what the being could be. Gramps thought hatchet Hands to be a man from the war who must have seen horrible things to make him lose his mind. Mrs. Hutchins disagreed, reminding Gramps about the unnatural foot tracks left by the intruder. Now, both were stumped. No clear understanding eased their minds. A point made, the only sightings were drawn by hunger.

Hatchet Hands is still seen from time to time at different farms on the mountain. What Hatchet Hands is remains a mystery. Its tracks have been followed into Spook Hollow, where the tracks fade and disappear. If Spook Hollow allows Hatchet Hands to live there, one can only assume its unnatural existence is a product of whatever force reins there.

Buckle Ridge

IT WAS A DRY SUMMER, hot and hazy. The sun beats steadily on, showing no mercy. Grass surrendered its emerald, green color, turning brown under the intensity of the midday sun.

Progress reached out, grabbing hold of the mountain. Familiarity was a comfort and change was unwelcome, but still it came.

An oil drilling company by the name of Dee & Dee drilling came to the mountain. Pennsylvania had always been rich in coal and oil. Deep in the mountains, a scout found the potential for a large oil strike. The drilling site was quickly set up. The site would work three shifts around the clock. A huge lighting system was positioned for night work.

News of the mountain change traveled fast. Many were unhappy with its invasion of progress, but still brought jobs. Art Hall was Gramps' best friend; he was experienced in running equipment. Gramps and Art sat on Morrelli's front porch. They were deep in conversation when an unfamiliar voice interrupted them. "Excuse me, one of you gents Art Hall?" Both men looked up. "My name is Henry Cooper, am a crew leader for the Dee & Dee." Gramps and Art stood, and all exchanged handshakes. Henry had heard talk about Art's skills with equipment. Art was offered a well-paying job for his skill. He was hired to run a bulldozer; his job would be to open new roads and expand the drilling site.

The sound of drilling equipment was heard 24 hours a day. Men worked hard and the boss pushed even harder. Progress came at a price.

Third shift had its advantages; pay was higher, and the temperature was cooler, more comfortable for working. However, after dark the site became eerie. The tree's shadows grew from the brightness of artificial light. The drilling vibrated every rock and boulder. Unexplainable happenings began.

Pipe that was stacked tumbled down for no reason. A work truck, parked for the night, had jumped into neutral then rolled towards the tents containing the sleeping crew. Coming to a sliding halt, the truck stopped inches short of the tents. Cries of a baby sounded through the darkness, waking all. A search group was sent out to look for the infant. When the men reached the limits of the light, the cries ended. On occasion, a mournful but urgent yell for help could be heard. No one could be found. Equipment would break down during the third shift. Mechanics would come to assess the machinery; they could find no problem. By morning, the equipment would run perfectly. The overnight crew, becoming spooked, one by one refused to work the early-morning shift. Eventually, third shift had to shut down.

With darkness came a cooler breeze, relief from the heat of the day. Twinkling stars littered a black sky. A quarter moon rose, providing little light. Art Hall ran a dozer second shift. He worked through the day and into the night. A new road was his job. Pushing through brush and rock, Art skillfully showed his talent. At 11:00 p.m., the crew leader signaled Art, the day shift was over, Art motioned for the boss. With only 20 feet remaining for completion, Art wanted to finish the push up to the huge boulder. Hesitantly, the boss agreed; after all, Art was experienced and really didn't need individual instruction. The remainder of the crew left the work site eager to leave after darkness fell.

Art, now alone with his machine, began working the dirt again. As Art approached the boulder, he checked his watch. 11:55, he was just about there when all the lights in camp came on. Art stopped the dozer. He stared at the camp illuminated by the lights. Curious, he jumped from the equipment, wanting to investigate. He walked the camp from corner to corner calling out. Deciding the lights have been on a timer satisfied Art. He returned to his work. The dozer pushed forward up against the large boulder. Art took a second run, this time jarring the rock forward. With a loud scream, a mountain of a man sprang up from the beaten ground. The being stood tall on the blade of the dozer. He stared at Art with piercing eyes. The man was wearing black trousers with a black shirt tucked in at the waist. His hair was groomed, hands placed on his hips, he tucked his chin to his chest, eyes still hard on Art. Moments passed in silence. Unable to hold ground, Art jumped from the running machine. He ran through the trees. Branches snapped back, whipping his face. The uneven ground didn't slow his pace.

Gramps was on the porch looking at the stars. He was restless tonight; sleep would not come. Gramps remembered Art would be working over in the next hollow. He drove over to meet him, and the conversation with coffee sounded good to Gramps.

Gramps drove the back roads with a knowing hand. He was familiar with each twist and turn. As he rounded a bend, he almost ran over Art. Art, breathless and wide-eyed, jumped in Gramps' truck. Struggling for air he managed to gasp, "Drive, Charlie Drive!" Gramps drove to Camp Mountain Run. In silence, they sat with only the purr of the engine. Gramps knew Art was not a skittish man; he was of solid character. Finally, Art began to unfold his story; he had Gramps; undivided attention.

Deciding they needed to tell the story to Henry, the crew boss, they drove into town. Reaching the motel, Art knocked on the door. It opened with a creek. Through a yawn, his boss asked, "What's up?" Art explained what had happened with the lights. Art's voice was shaky. Talking anxiously and fast, he told of a man that came from the ground. He described the events in detail. The boldness of the man dressed in black, almost transparent in sight. Gramps placed his hand on Art's shoulder; the pressure was reassuring. Art took a deep breath, exhaling slowly. Now wide awake, Henry knew he had to investigate. Not wanting to go alone, he awoke several other men to travel the mountain with him. Art refused to go back there. Gramps drove Art home, calming him with general conversation.

The drilling site was alive, the lighting was bright, the drilling rigs were digging, and Art's dozer was still pushing against the boulder. The group walked the grounds searching for a cause. There were no signs of the man dressed in black.

Events of that evening traveled from porch to porch. Somewhere between apprehensive, frightened of the unknown. Others, curious and doubtful. The drilling crew diminished, afraid to remain at work. Unable to employ a full crew, Dee & Dee made the decision to pull out. A skeleton crew only remained to fold up the site. The last day, they capped off the well. The cap was six feet around and six inches thick, made of solid cast iron.

Weeks had passed since the drilling crew pulled out. Talk of the company calmed. Gramps wanted another look at the site and hoped Dee & Dee had left the mountain in its natural state. He drove to the spot to have a look around. He saw the road Art had been moving. Gramps continued his inspection. The large well cap caught his eye. The thick cast iron had been twisted and torn off the well, then moved ten feet to the side. Perplexed, Gramps left the site to contact the drilling company. Without question, Dee & Dee sent equipment and manpower to recap the well. Again, a cast iron cap was placed over the well. Three-inch rivets were added to secure the cap.

A restlessness consumed Art. So many unanswered questions remained. He would make the drive to see Gramps. Talking would help. Gramps met Art with a warm smile and a firm handshake. With a welcoming slap on the shoulder, they entered into the kitchen. Gramps motioned towards a wooden chair positioned at the table. Art sat quietly, waiting while Gramps made a pot of coffee. Gramps carried on idle conversation, busying himself placing cups, sugar, and milk on the table.

Art began the conversation, "Well, Charlie, I don't know what to think." Gramps listened to Art express his concerns. Art stared into his coffee cup as he talked. The discussion between the two came to an understanding, answers were needed. Gramps suggested they travel to Clearfield to see Henry, the crew boss.

The drive gave time to soothe the worry Art felt. The hot sun replaced by a cooling fall brought relief. A hint of winter to come was evident. Brilliant colors had faded to rich rust, splashes of gold helped to brighten the mountains, and some bared their branches ready for sleep. Pines of green needles peaked above the others. Art remained quiet as he enjoyed the view. Gramps drove a steady pace toward town.

The town was alive with the rush of people in the street. Gramps greeted some with a tip of his hat. Art nodded his head in hello to passers-by. Black bold letters spelled out Dee & Dee on the office door. With a polite knock, Art and Gramps entered. Henry motioned for the men to come in and sit down. Henry sat at a large wooden carved desk. Papers and maps littered the desk. Gramps began the conversation focused on the happenings at the drilling site. Henry laid a map across his desk for Art and Gramps to see. The map detailed the mountain, and a see-through drawing of the drilling site was placed over the map. Gramps pointed to a spot with a skull and crossbones marked grave. The road Art was developing dozed through that area. Art sat back in his seat with a sigh.

Speechless, the men looked to one another. Instead of answers, new questions arose. Without satisfaction, Art and Gramps left the office. Art, more frustrated than before, suggested they look up the history of the mountain. Gramps drove to the town library. They gathered books of explanation. Each began researching. Gramps discovered in the late 1700, a rich family owned the mountain. They opened a mill and worked the mountain lands as a farm. The family was known as Bucklie's. They were a large group. Clayton Bucklie had eight children with his first wife, Mabel, and seven children with his second wife, Anna. Anna passed while giving birth to his last son. This was said to drive Clayton to madness. Reports told about an abusive father that was known for his explosive temper. The story told how the family's riches were dwindled away by a stubborn man that lived extravagantly. When the family lost their home and land, the insane owner murdered his entire family. He buried their bodies in one massive grave. He then burned down their home and outbuildings. It is believed Clayton in a mad state disappeared into the hollow never to be seen again.

Art and Gramps were stunned. A man living on their Mountain had done the unthinkable. They rode in silence as the truck rumbled home. Art was deep in thought about the yell for help, the baby's cry, the mourning of distress, and the grave pit, and had not realized Gramps drove past his house until the truck stopped.

Art, looking up, realized they were at the drilling site. Gramps told Art he wanted one more look around. Art exited the truck, he stood by the door looking around. Apprehensive about his surroundings, he looked from side to side. Gramps, seeing Art uncomfortable, came around to stand beside him. "Just a quick look around," Gramps said.

The two men walked through the drilling site, not looking for anything in particular. They came upon the well; Gramps stood and stared. Art followed Gramps' eyes. The well cap had again been removed. Something had ripped the twisted iron cap from the surface of the drilled well. Art shifted his weight back and forth. He nervously pulled on Gramps' shirt sleeve, signaling to leave. In a hurry to get out of there, both turned and headed towards the truck. A baby's cry sounded. Art broke out in a full run, Gramps fast on his heels. The doors slammed simultaneously. Dirt flew from the fast-exiting vehicle.

Once back, Gramps reported their findings of the cap being torn from the well again. The drilling company sent another crew up into the hollow. This time, dynamite was thrown into the well. A blast would seal the cap permanently, they hoped.

Gramps and Art avoided that area of the hollow. Sometimes, when they were out hunting, the sounds of a baby's cry would be heard.

The large man dressed in black was thought to be Clayton Bucklie, defending his property. A soul of unrest driven by madness. Violent in life, enraged in the afterlife. The cause?

Gramps always said, "Some things are better off not knowing."

Devil's Racetrack

THE DEVIL'S RACETRACK was a beaten path turned to dirt. It ran the ridge of Boone's Mountain then drops into a hollow. In a time of horse and wagon days, when settlers crossed the lands in search of the perfect life, this trail was the main route across Boone's Mountain. Many happy, hopeful faces had seen the beauty of the ridge. Mountain laurels bloomed a bright pink. The trees were a forest of green color. A time of faith, anticipation, and excitement, a new life was about to begin.

Days of travel started at dawn, wagons loaded, teams hitched. Heavy dust filled the air; a cloth tied around their faces made it easier to breathe. The weary travelers rested at night. Campfires provided light and safety from the wild. The evening meal was usually the hunt from earlier in the day.

Concerning stories of travel passed from the wagon train to the towns they journeyed through. Tails of livestock suddenly dying, water supplies becoming stagnant overnight, or a child becoming fatally ill, alarmed only a few. The promise of greener pastures was stronger than the fear of man's talk.

A wagon train traveling the trail had long, hard days. When night began to take over, the wagons were positioned for the rest. A grassy meadow looked to be a peaceful spot. Animals were cared for and supper was served. A central campfire was the main meeting ground. The men talked of the great fields and farms they would have once

they reached their destination. Excitement and laughter echoed through the camp. Children were tucked in for the night and women finished their chores.

Without warning the horses became restless' they pranced with low a winnie, pulling at their ropes of confinement, the group of men took notice. The fire gave a glow of light shining on the animals; no explanation was seen. A flickering fire of orange grew into a blaze of new heights. An ear-piercing roar shook the very ground from the center of the blaze, and sparks flew wildly. The gathering of men jumped back in amazement as the fire became enormous. A vile laugh spewed from the ashes; hot red coals flew as a serpent climbed out of the center. The scaled creature had long horns perched on top of its head. Claws of great lengths grew from its arms. A long beak sharp with huge, jagged teeth roared while smoke and flame shot from its nostrils. Its neck, long and scaled as a snake, had pointed bones spiking the back side. Another evil laugh released a foul odor to hang in the air. The Devil himself stood amid the flame. Swinging his neck from side-to-side, he glared at the group now proclaiming their wagon train to be trespassing on his ground. "If you remain, you will die!" the serpent hissed. In one quick motion, the creature grabbed one of the men, sinking claws into flesh, pulling the man into the center of the flame, a scream, and the man disappeared.

Women gathered their children; the young clung to their mothers with terror upon their cheeks. Men ran toward their wagons; shots rang out as some tried to shoot the creature. Bullets, having no solid target, continued a path through the serpent only to penetrate flesh of a settler on the other side. Chaos and confusion erupted running in all directions. Teams hitched; the wagon train escaped into the darkness. A vile laugh followed them through the hollow.

The settlers traveled throughout the night. Feeling safer now, wagons slowed to a normal pace. The outskirts of a town could be seen. The sun rose to greet a new day. Weary horses hung their heads in exhaustion. Townspeople stopped and stared as the wagon train entered. People cleared the street making room for the Travelers. Wagons continued through town to stop on the other side. Men helped their wives down from their seats. Children remained in the wagons for now. Adults gathered without conversation. Faces of somber glanced from eye to eye. A deep voice broke through the silence. "We need supplies." Heads nodded in response. Women gathered their children and headed to town. Men remained behind, caring for the animals and gathering firewood.

Dinner complete, the men gathered for conversation. Talking was hard. Events of the night before still weighed heavy. Unsure of all that had happened, talk began with questions. No explanations were offered. Drumming sounded the arrival of a horse rider entering camp.

A man dressed in a long, black coat and a smile on his face rode up to the group of men. He introduced himself as Preacher John while swinging a leg over the animal to dismount. the cheerful man had come to welcome the Travelers. Asking if all were well, he sensed a gloom within the group.

"Can I help?" the preacher asked. The group told of the events they had witnessed. Reliving it did not provide answers they sought. John took in their stories; he shook a knowing nod of his head. John had heard similar happenings from other mouths passed.

"The Hollow," Preacher John replied. "Unholy ground, an evil place without promise. Some place to avoid. Wickedness gathers there, never go back."

The travelers shifted in their seats; no more of an explanation would be provided. The trail became known as The Devil's Racetrack. A few still attempted to travel the route—some made it through, and some did not.

The HoDagg

SUMMER PAST HAD BEEN hot and dry. Harvest time was upon the mountain. Leaves now showing off their bright colors, winds blew, tossing an array of color into the wind. Each leaf danced its own twirling ritual as it floated towards the ground.

The forest ranger stood tall in the fire tower. Circumstances were favorable for fires to appear. The lookout tower stood on top of the mountain, overlooking the hollow. Ranger Tuck peered through his binoculars for signs of smoke. Trees carried a colorful blanket covering the mountain. Green pines peak through the mass of reds, oranges, and yellows. A movement caught his eye. Scanning closely, Tuck searched.

Tree branches parted, making room. Birds taking flight, their song announcing an intruder. He focused on a small clearing hoping to catch a glimpse. There stood a huge bear. It looked to be part bear, part horse. The creature was upright on hind legs with a long, thick tail holding the ground for balance. The creature released a resounding growl, dropped to all fours, disappearing into the thicket. Knowing the Scout camp was a few short miles ahead, Ranger Tuck decided to warn Gramps.

Hoping Gramps would not think him to be crazy, Tuck phoned. Gramps sat at the kitchen table sampling cookies Grandma had just made when the phone rang. The phone hung on the wall by the sink. Gramps pulled himself up, crossing the kitchen. "Hello," he answered. Gramps recognized Tuck's voice. The ranger told him of the strange sighting, believing it was heading towards the Boy Scout camp. Hodagg was back, thought Gramps. He thanked him as he pushed curtains back to look out his window. He kept watch for the remainder of the afternoon.

Night came without an event. It was a dark starry night with a crescent moon resting in the blackened sky. Gramps gave up his vigil with a yawn; he thought a drive would help to break the boredom. Gramps decided in the direction of Fawn Skin Bridge. The bridge crossed the stream that ran through Spook Hollow. Grandma decided to ride along just to get out and keep Gramps company. They drove toward Fawn Skin Bridge. Around a twisted turn, the bridge came into sight. There, in the center, consuming both lanes stood a huge Beast. It looked to be brown in color covered in thick, matted fur. Its eyes flashed a bright red, caught by the truck lights. Paws of iron clawed at the night, swiping viciously. A growl bared sharpened teeth as saliva dripped profusely from the corners of its mouth, its snout covered in blood. The Beast, upright on hind legs, started towards them. Grandma screamed, she was afraid. Gramps backed the truck up. The Beast kept coming; Grandma closed her eyes and prayed as a beast sounded another roar. Grandpa continued to back the truck up, but the Beast was gaining on them. He yelled for Grandma to hold on, thinking the Beast was charging the lights. Gramps would turn them off. Grandma opened her eyes only to be enveloped in darkness. With Grandpa's knowledge and skill of the road, he turned the truck around in the blackness. BANG! A savage jolt shoved the truck sideways. Grandma screamed again. The sound of metal being torn chilled Gramps to the bone. The truck now turned around with lights back on. They could see Hodagg angrily roar, throwing its head back and forth. Dropping to all fours, it challenged Gramps' truck once more. Screams of fright mixed with the winding engine of the truck, echoed in Gramps' head. With the truck now traveling forward, he could put distance between them. Grandma now sat closer to Gramps.

"What was that?" she asked, her voice still trembling. Gramps held her hand for reassurance. "Hodagg," he replied. Gramps explained the beast, a product of Spook Hollow. Stories told Hodagg was conceived with the Devil's hand. The fierceness of a mad grizzly bear combined with the speed of a stallion. The Beast would have no conscience and would hunt just for the kill. A pet to the devil, vile and cruel.

Once at home, Gramps walked Grandma in, his eye watching for a movement, in hopes Hodagg did not go the distance. Within the safety of home, Grandma relaxed with a cup of tea while Gramps sipped coffee, pacing from window to window. Gramps would keep watch throughout the night.

Days light, gray at first, brightened as time passed. Gramps had emptied the coffee pot during his night's vigil. After breakfast, he would travel to Merrile's General Store. Merrile's was a hum with shoppers and conversation.

Gramps was greeted by several as he stepped onto the porch. The first few minutes of small talk ended as Gramps cleared his throat. All eyes on him, Gramps told the events from last evening. Some whispered the name, "Hodagg." Grandpa Charlie told of his intentions to track the beast. A few shook their heads "No" and walked off the porch, not wanting to hear anymore. The others, remaining full of curiosity, would accompany Gramps.

The hunting party gathered at Gramps home. A group of well-armed neighbors loaded into trucks headed to Fawn Skin Bridge. Stopping short of the bridge, they spread out looking for signs of Hodagg. Tracks were found in the clay banks of the stream. Prints of the beast were five inches wide and 16 inches long. It had three toes to the front and a claw-like nail protruding from the outside. Prints were followed towards Gramps house then veered off. The hunting party followed.

Deeper into the woods, the tracks would lead them. Now at the mouth of Spook Hollow, the group hesitated. Gramps said anyone concerned could remain there to keep watch. All intent on the hunt, no one noticed the winds whipping the trees back and forth. The air, now cooler, was chilling. Tracks of the Beast were heavy at first, easy to follow. Further into the hollow the tracks began to fade, making them hard to see. The progress of the hunt slowed. Around a boulder, the tracks led once on the other side of the rock the tracks vanished. The group of men gathered around Gramps for direction. The hunt had come to an end. Heading home, the men noticed the rush of the trees but had no breeze on their face. At sunset, the group of men were wrapped in darkness. There was a need to escape Spook Hollow as quickly as possible. The night made travel more difficult. The hunters made their way over brush and rock. A long howl broke the silence. Gramps told everyone to remain calm; they were leaving the hollow.

The group moved quickly, a low growl caught in the darkness. The sound had no direction. Gramps told them to stay tight together. The hunters became the hunted. Guns ready, they continued in the direction of home followed by threatening growls all around them. Gramps lifted a hand to still the group movement. A twig snapped. Then another in the opposite direction. Not sure what circled them, Gramps had the men stand back-to-back, providing protection all around.

Gramps directed each man to take ten steps out and gather wood and twigs. On completion a large pile formed. Gramps explained he would build a fire to keep the creatures at bay. Fire would also provide necessary light. All eyes kept watch as Gramps built a fire. A vile screech sounded. Then commotion in the darkness where fire light could not reach, a long growl followed by a roar. Every man terrified, gun in hand, ready to act on a challenge. Gramps spoke softly to the men almost at a whisper. An encouraging "Keep calm" whisper. "Be prepared," he breathed. A noise like thunder in their chest, another roar. Eyes red aglow, moved through the night. Gramps occasionally would feed the fire, glowing ambers of orange danced upward floating in the night. A new day's dawn, the mist touched the ground. No sounds were heard for the hour past. Keen eyes watched as the fire was extinguished.

Gramps moved the group towards home; all had survived the night. Seated around Gramps' table, men were exhausted, drank coffee, and talked of their night. After a day's rest, a few wanted to trail the beast again. Adjusting and his chair, Grandpa Charlie shared his opinion. "I believe we need to let the unknown be, count our blessings. We need not challenge what stays in its own domain. If it becomes a threat, we will act." After some conversation, all agreed, as long as the mountain people were safe.

Hodagg's anger can still be heard sometimes on a clear night. Echoing through the valley, a warning not to enter the Hollow.

The Preacher

NIGHT OF DARK AND HUMID, air thick and heavy. Slivers of a silvery moon reflected brightly on smothering clouds. Camp Mountain Run was alive, engulfed with young scouts. All were seated around a large campfire. The flames flickered, dancing shadows off the trees. Gramps had their undivided attention as he unfolded the legends of Spook Hollow. Each was anticipating the next happening within the story. The Devil's Racetrack, Hatchet Hands, and the Hodagg were brought to life. Gramps kept his voice low, emphasizing certain details to captivate their minds.

Accompanying the scouts was Preacher Jacob. He was a tall, thin man that stood with a straight backbone. Stories told; the preacher held his Bible firm. He paced around the boys, shaking his head. Exhaling loudly, Jacob confronted Gramps. Preacher boldly walked up beside the fire. Ridged, he stood, voice full of conviction; he didn't believe in Spook Hollow, its creatures, or any other legend. The preacher stated his intentions to prove no such evil place was in existence. Demanding Charlie take him to the very spot, now, in the night. Gramps smiled, stood, and agreed, but would claim no responsibility.

The younger boys remained at the campfire, more secure near the light it provided. Gramps, Preacher, and two older teens began their adventure into the Hollow. Gramps called the older boys runners; their purpose being to run down new fleeing believers.

Spook Hollow, now in sight, winds began to pick up. Three hundred yards into the Hollow, a lightning storm struck. The storm was quick and furious in coming. Lightning flashed all around them. Crack of thunder echoed while the rumble shook you to your core. The light was blinding; its intensity was overwhelming. In a flash, an animal standing on its hind legs forty yards away roared, shaking its head from side to side. Gramps yelled "Hodagg!" and fired his rifle twice skyward to ward off the creature.

The Preacher, wide eyed, held his bible towards the beast. Another flash of lightning struck the trees beside them. Sparks flew, the sound of wings beating commotion and shrieks filled the sky. Prehistoric bird-like creatures swooped down from the trees. Again, lightning surrounded them. Hodagg, on its hind legs, was descending upon them.

In darkness, once again, Gramps fired another warning shot into the air. Fire flew from the gun barrel. More lightning bolts struck the ground and trees. The noise was intense. Fire grew from a downed tree. The anger of the storm continued with the next bolt of lightning. Gramps could see terror on the preacher's face. He was on his knees, looking up. The good book ripped with both hands, shaking the word of God toward the heavens. Gramps pulled the preacher to his feet. Jacob looked at Gramps' eyes, wide and stunned. The preacher yelled he believed. "I believe!" he repeated. "I believe there is something evil in this hollow." He had grabbed Gramps by both arms, shaking him as he spoke. Then the preacher turned and ran. He ran so fast, the runners could hardly keep up. The flashes of light provided eyes upon him as he ran back to the scout campfire. He didn't stop but continued running to his car; the preacher yelled out his window, he would not stay there, not one night. Gramps smiled with an understanding. Spook Hollow had a new believer.

Sky Walker

A TROPICAL DAY, the morning already humid and hot, Gramps worked the garden, sweat dripping from his brow. Crops would be plentiful this harvest. A peaceful morning, Gramps thought. Bird of song, sang a merry tune. The hoe breaking ground with each powerful swing gave rhythm to the morning melody. Insects buzzed themselves, doing what bugs do. From the back porch, Grandma gave a yell, a cold glass of lemonade in her hand. Grateful for the break, Gramps smiled, heading in her direction. The rumble of a truck made Gramps turn to see his neighbor, Jonas, pulling up the drive. Grandma went to get another lemonade. Gramps greeted Jonas. Both men sat on the porch cooling themselves.

Jonas had a purpose for his visit. "Charlie, I have a problem. Gramps sat up, intent on listening. Jonah spoke of his ranch with a proud gleam in his eye. He raised cattle, great beasts of size with long horns and thick, brown coats. Jonas began by hanging his head. "My cattle have been attacked by something," he said, looking up now. He explained the young lie dead, picked apart by something. The large, older cattle were bloodied, their backs raw with open flesh. Jonas could hear fearful bellowing from his cattle. He rushed to their pens only to see the horror he had described. No sign of the cause, Gramps adjusted in his chair, deep in thought. He would have to investigate.

Together, they journeyed to the ranch. The scene before them was a horrid site. Gramps looked about, no tracks, no markings, absent of clues. Gramps, without answers, suggested a visit to Merrilli's General Store.

An intense game of checkers was in play. Gramps and Jonas joined the group without notice.

The opponents, caught up in the win, unaware of the new arrivals, continued their fight. Upon the game's end, Grant spoke his greetings. He stated he had come with concerns, explaining the findings at Jonas' ranch. All remained quiet, eyes looking from person to person. Suggestions from coyotes to bears were spoken. Jonas explained there were no ground tricks. A plan developed to guard their neighbor's livestock that night.

Dust came with a gleam of orange enveloped by the darkening sky. Men positioned throughout the ranch waiting, their guns loaded. ready to defend. Moon glows against a velvet night quiet except for the lull of the resting cattle. A few men dozed, propped upright against the animal stalls. Gramps sat on the front porch, his chair tipping back against the inner wall. Through the darkness. he could see the silhouettes of others waiting, watching. His mind drifted peacefully. The rush of wind caressing his face brought his mind back. Easing the chair back on all fours, Gramps stood, looking for its cause. Shadows flickered past the moon's light. A shriek set the night into movement. Men appeared in search of the sound. Whooshing air sounded close to their heads. The predator was in flight. Wings beating, rushing, air stirring the dust. The cattle now panicked, bellowed, and paced in their stalls. Men ran for cover.

The creatures were huge, possibly a 12-foot wingspan, long, pointed beaks lined with teeth. Claws clean edged on webbed feet descended upon the animals, shredding flesh with the sharp of their beak. The bawl of the cattle instilled fear in all living beings.

Gramps stood amongst the commotion; he fired his shotgun skyward. He discharged his weapon again. The creatures disappeared as quickly as they came. All gathered in the barnyard. Jonas sought care for his cattle.

Grant spoke calmingly to the group, keeping their surge of alarm subdued. He explained the threat was over for now; the men should return home to check on their own families and property. He would make a few inquiries, and all could join him at his home at Camp Mountain Run in three hours.

The drive down the mountain was without event. A new day welcomed the rise of the sun, its warming rays drying the morning dew. Gramps knew who he needed to talk to. Jobe was an old-timer whose family had come into existence at the mountain base; they had always been there as far back as anyone could remember.

Gramps drove the distance until the road's end; he would finish the trip on foot. Jobe lived a spell beyond the road's reach. Still early morning, Gramps hoped to catch Jobe before the day's hunt.

Jobe met Gramps as he climbed the steps to the front porch. With a grin and a chuckle, he shook Gramp's hand, motioning him towards a chair. Jobe was of good size; he must have been a mountain of a man and his younger days. He stood six foot and three inches tall. He carried broad shoulders and a hand as large as a grizzly bear.

After their polite greeting, Gramps told the accounts of last night and of Jonas' ranch. Jobe sat back, eyes remembering an earlier time. Minutes passed; Gramps knew to wait. With a sigh, Jobe leaned forward. "Awful creatures, aren't they." Gramps responded with a nod. Searching for words of memory, Jobe scratched his head. "Yeah, long ago we called them sky walkers, usually looking for food," was Jobe's answer. "The hollow is their home. Curious creatures that from time to time do attack humans." He told of a sky walker's attack on a young teen hunting. The boy had fallen to the ground while retrieving his kill. Sky walker leaped upon him while he was down. The creature slashed the boy's jugular vein with its long toenail. Gramps listened to the gruesome tail without words. Jobe explained to rid themselves of them. "Keep all livestock closed in a barn and keep all children in

their homes. Sky walkers did not like loud noises. Bang pots and pans, shout and fire your guns." He explained, "Do not hit or hurt them, they will come back and dive again. Skywalkers have the ability to remember human faces and will warn others about you. Protect your head and take cover," Jobe explained. "They will come and search, at feeding time, they will fly in silence swooping low, if they find nothing, they would leave just the same in silence. After a few nights of this, they will leave and not return to that spot."

Gramps listened to the old-timer's advice. After Jobe finished, Gramps asked if they could be hunted. "Better to let them exist in the hollow," Jobe replied. "Sky walkers have a way of remembering your face, then you would become the hunted."

Gramps took his conversation back to the waiting group. Some still wanted to hunt them; others agreed to hide their livestock. Upon nightfall, neighbors locked their barn doors, and windows were latched tight. Gramps turned the lights down low. He sat at the table, staring into his coffee cup. A swish of forced air rattled the window glass in its pane. Gramps turned off the lights. He stood to the side of the window, cautiously peering from side to side. Only the moon's light provided a shadow of the creature's presence. Gramps watched them circle the barnyard. Just as Jobe had said, after a few minutes, the sky walkers disappeared.

The next two nights were the same; sky walkers would silently appear, circle the area, and then be gone. Neighbors met daily to discuss the night before. Everyone had the same happenings.

The fourth night, the sky walkers did not circle the skies, no signs of them at any homestead. The remainder of the week was without event. Concerns eased and life went back to normal. Sky walkers, a bird-like creature, a mystery of Spook Hollow, keep watch on the skies.

Conclusion

CREATURES OF THE MOON, shy in sun's ray. In darkness, evil dances. In light, angels sing. Silence is calming, while screams fear bring. Spook Hollow in day to blind eye is enchanting, a mystical beauty of nature's gift. Shadow of night surrounds all good things. The gray is a settlement between dream and awareness, safety or harm. In darkness, unseen danger, mixed with enchantment of unhallowed realm, a feeling of unrest. Spook Hollow, a real place, true state of mind, or just imaginary? Visit this place, but only for self-assurance. Once authenticity presents itself, heed the warning. Life will never return to ordinary. Exhausted from discovery, rest will come slowly. Eyes flutter to stay open for the blackness releases the myth. Your bedroom door deliberately closes the latch clicks softly, finalizing what fear is made of.